I0716315

Unforgettable Christmas

Stella Williams

Serpentine Creative LLC

Copyright © 2024 by Stella Williams

All rights reserved.

No portion of this book may be reproduced in any form without written permission from the publisher or author, except as permitted by U.S. copyright law.

Cover Art by Covers in Color www.coversincolor.com

Edited by Raw Book Editing

Contents

Run, Rudolph, Run

Trishelle

Trishelle Harris shimmied to the left before dropping to one knee and blowing a kiss to her camera. With a final wink, she finished the last take of the latest internet dance trend. It may have taken her about thirty takes to get it perfect all the way through, but she'd done it. Now she just needed to edit it for some razzle-dazzle and additional Christmas flair and she'd be ready to upload it. Unfortunately, because of the extra takes, it would have to wait until after her day job duties. Corporate real estate was not for the weak but gave her the funds and free time to focus on her true passion. She spread the joy of Christmas to the world via their smartphones and computer screens.

She picked up her phone to see how much time she had left to change from her online persona Holly J. Trishmas to Trish Harris, the professional and cursed. There was no time to change if she didn't want to be late. Her trendy industrial condo in the up-and-coming warehouse district of Mulberry was twenty minutes from downtown without traffic. Now, during peak after-hours lounge time, it would take her at least an extra twenty minutes. Meaning her prosthetic ears and emerald green velvet corset top minidress would have to stay, but she kicked off her candy stripe tights, mistletoe-topped elf hat, and tinsel-toed heels, swapping them for sensible black pumps and an oversized black blazer.

She winced as she rushed past the full-length mirror in the hall on her way out the front door. She looked like she was making a mad dash away from a holiday party one-night stand, but being late to a meeting with Kevin Kerrigan was not going to happen. Besides the fact that dude was a major creep and would probably get a kick out of her outfit, he was also the head of one of the largest hotel chains in the country and making a deal with him for new properties would solidify her as a top agent, even if she was just a junior realtor working the account.

Sure, she could have parlayed her friendship with Sinai Carlisle into a deal with Sinai's boyfriend Dominic Westmore, but Trishelle had never been one to take the easy route when it came to her success. She wanted to earn her accomplishments on her own steam. Even if that meant dealing with who some in prominent circles considered the devil. She had already used up a favor to get into one of Dom's redesigned warehouse condos for half the going price and a cross-promotional publicity blitz on her socials.

Trishelle blasted Mariah Carey's All I Want For Christmas Is You and dialed up the Sugar Plum air freshener in her holiday red Acura sedan to calm her nerves as she sped like a madwoman through the streets of Mulberry. They were, of course, meeting Mr. Kerrigan at K Hotel's popular rooftop lounge. Kevin Kerrigan was as much a party boy as he was a feared businessman. Pulling up to K Hotel with five minutes to spare, Trishelle splurged on valet parking and thanked the heavens K Hotel's elevators were fast and smooth.

The lounge had started filling up with the post-work drink crowd but Trishelle spotted her boss, Kelly Green, right away. He was hard to miss in his signature green blazer, and when he spotted her, she could tell right away she was in trouble. His pale face turned splotchy and red, his already thin lips disappearing altogether as he took in her attire. Unconsciously, her pace slowed. This wasn't the first time she'd pissed off Mr. Green, but without her social media expertise, he'd have been passed over years ago as younger more internet-savvy realtors had flocked to Mulberry's burgeoning high-end real estate market. That meant as much as they disagreed about certain things, she felt her job was fairly safe.

That knowledge bolstered her confidence enough to get her to the table with a smile on her face. Ignoring her simmering boss, Trishelle put on her networking hat and greeted the man of the hour at his side.

"Normally I'd demand an apology for keeping me waiting, but this outfit," Kevin Kerrigan's black gaze slid up and down her body and Trishelle fought the urge to squirm and flee from his scrutiny, "was certainly worth the wait."

He might have only used his eyes to undress her, but she swore it felt like slimy black tendrils of sleaze were racking their way across her flesh.

"Thank you, I do apologize," she said, hoping her voice didn't come out as meek and uncomfortable as it sounded to her ears.

"Don't fret, Ms. Harris, if you were late, I'm sure we could still come to an agreement that would satisfy both of our needs," he said before gesturing for her to take the seat next to his.

Every cell in Trishelle's body protested the idea of getting any closer to Mr. Kerrigan, so instead, she chose the seat next to Mr. Green. Dealing with his anger was a far sight better than subjecting herself to come-ons from Mr. Kerrigan. She may be able to hold her composure from afar, but if he touched her? She would have no control over her reaction and knew it wouldn't be good.

"Speaking of arrangements, let's get to business," Mr. Green jumped in, saving Trishelle from having to respond to Mr. Kerrigan's blatant come-on.

Trishelle listened intently to Mr. Green's pitch, making sure he hit the key points Trishelle had highlighted for him in her report about Mr. Kerrigan and what his goals were in expanding his empire. She jumped in here and there when she felt Mr. Green wasn't quite hitting the mark. It didn't seem to matter, though. Mr. Kerrigan seemed distracted by Trishelle's attire. Even going so far as to blatantly stare at her enhanced cleavage and lick his lips. If she was worried that her attire might ruin the deal, she'd been wrong. It was clear, to her at least, Mr. Kerrigan had already made up his mind and Kelly Green Realty would not be getting the contract, but he was entertaining Mr. Green as a way to prolong his interaction with her.

Never in her life had Trishelle ever felt so unsafe while working as a realtor. Not even when she worked the flipping circuit with her ex-boyfriend and dealt with nearly condemned buildings, squatters, and other house pests daily. As soon as Mr. Kerrigan signaled he was done with Mr. Green, she hightailed it out of there right along with him, despite Mr. Kerrigan's suggestion she stick around for after-work mingling.

"That guy was such a creep. If he already knew he wasn't interested in our proposal, he should have said so from the beginning instead of wasting our time," Trishelle said.

"Of course, he wasn't interested in our proposal with you dressed like a Christmas tart," Mr. Green snapped.

Trishelle's gaze snapped to her boss, who was now shaking with rage.

"Are you mad that he was too much of a lech to pay attention to your pitch or mad that using me as bait didn't work?"

She was pissed off, too. Not just for him calling her a tart, but for insisting she join this meeting under the guise of it being a teaching opportunity. A chance to move up in the ranks. She'd not listened when the other female realtors warned her; hell, even Sinai who had her reasons to dislike Kevin Kerrigan had advised her not to go and now she knew why. It was never for her benefit to go. She'd merely been a carrot to dangle in front of the city's most notorious playboy.

"How dare you try to turn this debacle on me. We didn't get this account because of your lack of professionalism. If I wanted to throw Kerrigan a bone, you would certainly not have been my first choice. Don't bother coming to work tomorrow. You, Ms. Harris, are not Kelly Green material!"

Trishelle gawked at her boss as he stormed off the elevator. Did he just fire her? After she was sexually harassed all night for his contract? Without thinking, Trishelle reached into her bag, grabbed her Kelly Green Realty employee pin, and followed him. When she caught up to him, she slammed the pen into his chest. It was by pure coincidence it happened to be positioned pointy side out when she did, and she immediately cringed seeing it was now stuck in his chest.

The whole lobby went silent, aside from Mr. Green howling in pain and threatening to have her locked up for assault. It had been an accident, but in the heat of the moment, Trishelle had no qualms letting him think it was intentional as she marched out to the valet.

Jesse

Eleven pairs of doe eyes stared expectantly at Jesse as he waltzed through the family stables, but he ignored them all. If his family wanted to have a chat with him about his latest mood, they would have to revert to their human forms and pry the noise-canceling earbuds out of his ears with their hands.

He whistled to himself, enjoying the silence they provided. Santana, California wasn't exactly a quiet mountain town. The town proper was a giant playground for holiday fanatics. Unlike most towns that were content to focus on one event a year to celebrate their favorite holiday, the folks in Santana had decided that not only could they not pick just one, but it needed to be a year-round extravaganza to keep the tourists coming year-round. Somehow, no one ever thought being a quiet supply hub and access point to the most majestic mountain hikes in the warmer months and snowy hideout close to the more popular ski resorts in the winter months was a worthy pursuit.

In his youth, the bright lights and holiday cheer had been magic. The ability and safety to traverse town in whatever form he cared to inhabit felt freeing. Now as an adult, he was annoyed with the disrespectful, entitled tourists with their cameras, their demands, and just basic disregard for the rules set in place to ensure the humans and shifters in the area could coexist without toes being stepped on or heads being bitten off, both figuratively and literally.

He was just about finished building his private cabin further up the mountain. Close enough to still be near his family and the pack, but far enough away not to have to deal with the constant holiday music blasting from the town speaker system and the excited or frightened shrieks of children and adults alike when they encountered a free-roaming shifter unexpectedly. Yeah, he was ready for some quiet, the kind one got when out in the real wild, not the manufactured silence his earbuds provided but would have to do for now.

Jesse made his way to the front office of Santa's Workshop, the unfortunately named family business, to find his mother leaning way too close to the computer screen on her desk as she scrolled through holiday-themed social media content. She looked up when he walked into the room and started talking, but he couldn't hear a word she said.

Reluctantly, he pulled his tiny salvation out of his ears and winced as his eardrums were blasted with Elmo and Patsy singing Santa Got Runover By A Reindeer. Jesse was one reindeer who would love to run Santa over if it meant he never had to hear this song again. It was jokingly the family anthem because when they had first arrived in Santana some hundred years ago, their wagon had run over the town Santa that Christmas. Also the town drunk, the idiot had decided to nap under the wagon wheels and no one noticed till they'd broken both his legs. The family had only been passing through, but had stayed in town to make up for the accident. Long story short, Jesse's family had revolutionized Christmas in Santana and was arguably the reason it had become the monstrosity of a holiday haven it was today.

"Ma, I didn't hear a word you said!" he shouted over the music.

"No need to yell! I was just saying you need to clean up all the reindeer poop you just tracked inside," she huffed and turned her attention back to her screen.

Jesse looked down at his boots and scowled. Sure enough, shitty boot prints led from the back door into the office. Sure, he had been the one to track it inside, but the only reason there was poop on his boots was because one of the younger reindeer hadn't cleaned up after themselves like a good little shifter. Maybe that was why they had been ogling him oddly in the stalls earlier. They'd seen him walk through some poop and the little shits hadn't said a thing. Not that he would have heard them if they had. Either way, the whole lot was going to get an earful from him. It was bad enough he was saddled with the job of head reindeer this year because Pa hadn't found a full-time replacement for Santa yet, despite several locals expressing interest.

To be fair, Jesse agreed with his father that Mr. Carlisle was the man for the job. However, he would be away this season visiting his twin daughters, who, like most of the human children raised in Santana, hit the road as soon as they graduated Santana High. Amaya and Sinai had been amazing dancers, they'd even starred in one of those teen dance movies once, but last he heard, Amaya was in banking out Sowell Gate way and Sinai was a party planner in Mulberry. Maybe he should have followed the trend and left Santana for college instead of completing an online degree. His parents wouldn't have batted an eyelash if he had declared he'd wanted to leave to find a mate. Yeah, that would have been an easy out of all the holiday madness, but there was one thing about Santana he wouldn't be able to get anywhere else. His family was one, and the freedom to roam in whatever form was comfortable was another. Not exactly many reindeer habitats left and even fewer with as much protection as Santana. So yeah, while he was admittedly the town grinch, Santana was home.

Hell, even being single wasn't an issue. He had plenty of tourists to satisfy his base needs without the complication of a relationship, and if he ever decided he wanted to settle down, there were annual shifter gatherings he could attend in the hopes of finding his fated mate. He was a simple man, and as long as the attraction was there and they had a healthy relationship with holidays, he was golden. Jesse wasn't there yet, though. Otherwise, he may have settled for his last girl-friend, who still swung through town during the busy season to help out her family. Right now, he had poop to clean. He walked back to the door and kicked off his boots before grabbing the mop and broom to clean up the mess.

Out of the corner of his eye, he watched his mom as she continued scrolling, occasionally stopping to scribble down notes on her legal pad. Jesse usually didn't get involved with the business side of things, despite his parents' insistence that he learn as the oldest and next in line to take over Santa's Workshop. However, the last time he'd caught his Ma scrolling like this, she'd forced the family to wear sparkly leotards and do a silly dance she swore was all the rage and Jesse had ended up spending a good chunk of his reno budget getting his tech-savvy cousin to erase all videos and pictures of him in the stupid costume from the internet. He still got a few suspect stares from tourists now and again, but it was worth it. No one needed to see that ever.

"Ma, what shenanigans are you up to now?" Jesse grumbled, marching over to her desk.

He noticed she was in the messaging app with someone called Holly J. Trishmas before she clicked out of the program and grinned at him.

"Hopefully, I've just solved some of our staffing problems," she sighed.

"Say what now?"

"Don't worry your little head about it, Jesse. We all know you don't want anything to do with the details. Just know that by this time next week, we should have a new head elf to train up for the season."

"I'm not mad about filling some open positions, but I don't like the idea of bringing in an outsider," Jesse said.

"I'm not either, but at this point, we are out of options and Sinai Carlisle personally recommended this one. Besides, I have a good feeling about my choice. Just wait and see," Ma said.

Jesse snorted, "Yeah, I'll just have to wait and see."

He left his mother at her work and headed to rinse off his work boots.

Trishelle

Not even binge-watching the Santa Clause movies while destroying her stash of emergency holiday snacks had helped her sour mood. Of course, she was fired, but thank God, Mr. Green had decided not to press charges for her accidental assault last night. Although, the trip to the police station this morning had been totes fun. She would have to do something big for Sinai when she could afford to do so. Her friend hadn't hesitated to use her Westmoore connections to get Trishelle out of a situation that could have been infinitely worse. The twenty minutes she spent in holding had been eye-opening. She'd questioned everything about her life that led up to that point, and well, she hadn't liked what she'd become.

For one, she realized she was a mediocre real estate agent. Like, she was pretty and charismatic, which went a long way, but her heart wasn't in it. What she wanted wasn't a career in real estate. Unfortunately, her career as an influencer wasn't going to pay the bills, and it would take more than a little Christmas magic to replenish her bank account from her latest supply restock. She'd been counting on the commission from another sale to do that. Now she would have to dive into her DMs to see if any of the brand deals she passed up on before were still open to collaborating with her. Many weren't paid deals but ones offering products for her to feature and keep for free.

Back at home, Trishelle was just about to give up and start polishing her resume for maybe a gig being a social media manager when a new DM hit her inbox. She couldn't help the smile that lit her face when she read that it was from Santa's Workshop. She'd been following them ever since Sinai had put her on to them a year or so ago. The cute family-owned business was based in Sinai's hometown, Santana, California, the mecca for holiday lovers. Their content featured mostly slice-of-life content surrounding their reindeer farm and promo for their Christmas-themed shows. She would love a collaboration with them, even if it wasn't paid.

She opened the DM and nearly choked on her Little Debbie Holiday Cake. Inside wasn't just an offer to collaborate. They were offering her a full-time job as Head Elf, complete with decent pay, room, and board. She nearly dropped her phone as she squealed and did a happy dance around her living room. If she had been feeling sad about her life before, it barely registered to her dopamine-filled brain then. Without a second thought, she typed out her acceptance of the offer. Within the hour, she was talking directly with the owner, Mable "Ma" Freeman, and finalizing details. Then she called Sinai to thank her profusely for saving her butt a second time in twenty-four hours. By that time the following day, she was tossing her necessities into her Acura and hitting the road for Santana.

It's Beginning To Look A Hot Mess Christmas

Jesse

Climate change was kicking his butt. It was only 8 a.m. and the temperature in the stables had already hit at least the 80s. He scowled, thinking about the crazy snow that had hit the year prior and how he'd actually prayed for warmer weather. Looked like the joke was on him. He marched down Main Street, decorated with its Christmas hat wearing flamingos and peppermint beach balls for Christmas in July. The town speakers played a calypso version of jingle bells, and that just made his mood worse since someone had thought it funny to hide his earbuds so he couldn't have a moment's peace while in town. He needed coffee and for the first time in his life, he might order it iced with the way the sweat rolled down his back and pooled in the hem of his shorts.

Thankfully, Jingle Bell Java wasn't far from Santa's Workshop and their Holly Jolly Jumbo Ice Java would cure some of his morning crank before he had to meet with Ma and their new hire. Ms. Trishmas had arrived sometime last night, and Ma had been yacking his ear off all morning about how perfect she seemed for the job. Another reason he was braving the tourist area to get his coffee instead of grabbing some from the break room.

The tourists weren't quite out and about at this hour, but the heat had driven most of them to the indoor attractions and restaurants. This meant instead of a quick trip to grab some liquid mood booster, he was stuck in line waiting for the indecisive tourists to decide if they wanted a Gingerbread Mochachino with the peppermint sprinkles or with the reindeer munch crunch. After almost ten minutes of the couple in front of him hemming and hawing over their choice only to order with many substitutions and changes, he could almost see Marguerite, the shop owner and this morning's head barista, start sweating that he was about to lose his stuff.

"Come on, people, there's a line here," he snapped before he could stop himself. The couple turned to glare at him, and he glared right back.

The man had the nerve to push his wife behind him and square up like he wanted to fight. Jesse rolled his eyes and shook his head.

"That will be thirty twenty-five," Marguerite said, breaking into their stare down. The tourist guy's head whipped around to face her instead.

"Excuse me?"

"That will be thirty twenty-five," Marguerite repeated.

"For two coffees? That's insane!" the man said, turning his ire on the deceptively fragile-looking older woman.

"You ordered two large Gingerbread Mochachinos with at least 10 substitutions and add-ons, which cost extra, so yes, thirty twenty-five is your total. Will that be cash or card?" Marguerite said.

This wasn't her first rodeo dealing with tourists, and Marguerite was anything but a wilting flower. She was THE Mother Bear of the Santana Bears. The tourist was lucky it was early and Marguerite's sons weren't there. Affectionately nicknamed the Wee Bears, they acted as the muscle around town, making sure unruly tourists were dealt with quickly and quietly.

The couple looked between Marguerite and Jesse, and he could see the man's pulse jumping in his neck. Yeah, he wasn't going to just get his coffee and go.

"This is highway robbery! You all market this place like a fairy tale land full of happy holiday spirit, and yet you," he pointed at Jesse, "are the definition of a grinch, and you," he pointed at Marguerite, "are a…"

"Excuse me!" A voice like sweet honey called from behind Jesse.

Delicate fingers brushed his arm as the hottest fucking elf he had ever seen slid around him. Dressed in a green velvet mini dress with red silk trim and matching pointy slippers, the elf hit him about chest level in height. She smelled of warm cinnamon and sugar plums, and she was waving her free hand toward the phone in her other hand. The phone was pointed directly at the tourist, and from Jesse's vantage point, he could see she was streaming live to over 300 people.

"Don't threaten me with your phone. I bet you don't even have your camera open," the guy scoffed.

"Oh no, sir, this isn't about you. I'm just trying to share this wonderful menu with my gracious followers and your tirade is unfortunately not the content I want to provide. You see, Santana is a very special place and you are ruining the fantasy with your childish tirade. We wouldn't want to be on Santa's naughty list, would we? I mean, berating this lovely small business owner over prices you wouldn't bat an eyelash at in a bigger city," her tone stayed smooth and sweet but there was an underlying threat there; Jesse could feel it like an icicle falling from a roof.

The guy scowled at the little elf before throwing up his hands. "To hell with this place. Come on, honey, I'll take you to Paris next month," he snapped and stormed off, dragging his partner with him. The elf woman watched him go before turning her camera around to her face, and he nearly tipped over trying to get a better look at her on the phone screen. He'd judged her hotness based on her curvy little body, but seeing her face. He licked his lips and wondered if she'd blast him on social media if he asked if she were open to riding a reindeer.

"And that, ladies and gentlemen, is all I have for today. This elf needs to get her coffee in quick before her first shift at Santa's Workshop!" With that, she wiggled her nose and winked before ending the live.

Jesse was so awestruck he almost didn't notice that she had cut him in line until Marguerite was already taking her order.

"Hey! I was here first," he complained.

Marguerite and the intriguing little elf both shot him a look.

"Sorry, but I really am in a hurry," the elf said.

"Don't worry about him, love, and drinks are on the house for handling that Picky Pete for me."

"Oh, thank you! It was no problem. I dealt with plenty of difficult men in my life," the elf said.

Jesse did not like the sound of that, but he also didn't like that Marguerite was siding with this outsider. Especially when she had cut him in line.

"Aren't you worried about being on Santa's naughty list for cutting me in line?" he asked.

The elf wrinkled her nose, and it was so adorable. Hell, he hadn't thought anything as adorable since the last round of new calves had been born almost a year ago. Then she did the unthinkable. She sidled up to him and tugged on his shirt until he bent down to her eye level. Yeah, he actually did that, bent so he could be eye to eye with her chocolate depths. Her sweet scent overwhelmed him and made him feel all warm and gooey in the middle, like a freshly baked chocolate brownie.

"Would you believe me if I said I had an in with the big man?" she giggled before booping his nose.

"Sweetheart, you can have an in with this big man anytime you want," he found himself saying.

She did that little nose wiggle and wink before she turned to collect her drink from Marguerite. He watched like a helpless baby lamb as she took a sip of her drink and moaned while shimmying in delight. The tiny bells sewn onto the red silk lapels of her outfit jingled and jangled, and his dick got rock hard.

"See you around, Big Man," she said before sauntering out the door.

With a shake of his head, Jesse turned back to Marguerite, who smirked and held out an Iced Holly Jolly Jumbo Java to him.

"Pay me later. Go get your tourist, Big Man," Marguerite laughed.

Part of Jesse wanted to protest Marguerite's astute observation, but it had been a while since he'd last had a good fling and the little elf had inspired a previously unknown kink. You would have thought he'd have had his fill of naughty elves, but considering his family business, never before had it been sexy to him. At least, not before her.

"Thanks, Marg!" he called before running out the door.

Trishelle

Heaven was definitely a place on Earth and that place was Santana, California. Driving up to the city at night had done it little justice. The cute gingerbread cottages on Main Street were more perfect in person. The cute Jingle Bell Java was her new favorite place, not to mention the cute grinch she might have the opportunity to show the Christmas spirit to later. Oh yeah, she was sure she'd made the right choice to accept the offer to work at Santa's Workshop and she hadn't even started yet.

She smiled as she took in the Christmas in July theme. The extremely well-trained real-life flamingos stood proudly in the town fountain balancing sunglasses on their beaks and kicking around peppermint beach balls with their long spindly legs. The hidden speakers played a calypso version of Jingle Bells, further setting the beach vibe. She sipped her Santa's Secret Iced Mocha and once again swooned over the delicate balance of coffee and chocolate, and she was pretty sure Santa's Secret was coconut rum, non-alcoholic, of course.

What made it even better was the fact no one looked at her crazy for being dressed like an elf. No one surreptitiously filmed her to make fun of her online or made snooty comments about her missing the cosplay convention by several months. Even the overheated morning couldn't kill her jovial mood. She felt like she'd found home and she hoped it stayed that way.

"Excuse me! Hey! Wait up!" A male voice called from behind her.

Trishelle smirked to herself before turning to see "Big Man" jogging toward her, his own much larger iced coffee clutched in his hands. The man was an enigma; he was tall and definitely had muscles, but he was so graceful and almost delicate in his movements. He was beautiful loping after her like a gazelle on the prairie. Yet what she had gleaned about his personality was anything but delicate and smooth. He was harsh, and dare she say, hostile. A grinch of the highest order, which seemed fitting for a town so full of holiday cheer. She could just imagine him in some mountain cabin, glaring down at the town and shaking his fist at the tourists and the caroling.

"Why should I?" she laughed.

"Why should you what?" he asked, slowing as he got closer.

"Wait for you? I wasn't lying when I said I have an appointment," she said before taking another long sip of her liquid daydream.

The sun beat down relentlessly on her, as if intentionally trying to simulate the fires of passion she wished to stoke with the man. Later, just not right now, when she was supposed to be mentally preparing for her first day of work.

He nodded. "I'm headed to Santa's Workshop myself. I can make sure you get there without being bothered by any more disgruntled tourists."

The snort of laughter that escaped her shot the last sip she'd taken of her coffee straight up her nose and out in such a spit-take fashion it would have been comical if it hadn't sprayed all over the front of her dress and his shirt. He jumped back, and Trishelle covered her mouth, mortified.

"Oh my god! I am so sorry," she gasped when she was able to catch her breath.

The guy looked down at his shirt and scowled before setting his drink on the edge of the fountain and stripping it off. Trishelle dropped her hand, her mouth agape at the sight before her. Golden brown skin glistening in the sun, she watched as sweat and remnants of her coffee trailed down the plateaus and valleys of his six-pack before disappearing into the waistband of his shorts.

When she forced her gaze back up to his face, he grinned at her with the most adorable lopsided smirk. "You sure you didn't do that on purpose to see me half naked?"

"Um..." For once in her life, Trishelle was speechless. No witty comeback came to mind, and while she should be mortified, she was far too gone in her attraction to care at the moment.

He picked his drink back up, and she watched intently as his tongue encircled the straw before his full lips clamped shut over the plastic tip. His cheeks hollowed slightly as he sucked, and while she was captivated by his mouth, she felt his stare travel over her body.

"If we weren't in the middle of town, I'd suggest you show me yours, but for now, let's get you to the workshop. We can get you cleaned up, and I'll give you a private tour," he said before tossing his arm over her shoulder and directing her down the street toward her workplace. It took a moment for her brain to process his words, and by the time it did, he was already pushing the doors open to Santa's Workshop. The sudden temperature drop from the blasting AC brought Trishelle back to Earth. That and the smiling older woman behind the front desk.

"Oh good, you found her! I thought I might have to send a search party out to find our new hire. You know how overwhelming the first few days in Santana can be," the woman addressed Trishelle's shirtless companion.

He quickly dropped his arm from her shoulder and put distance between their bodies.

"Our new hire?"

Trishelle watched as his teasing smile from earlier melted away to a look of abject horror. Apparently, the woman saw it too as she looked between the two of them.

"Oh dear! Jesse, were you trying to get in her pants already? Listen, you're an adult and I usually stay out of your business with the ladies, especially the tourists, but you know how hard it is to find an outsider to help around here," the woman began.

Now it was Trishelle's turn to study them both. She saw similarities in that they shared similar coloring and wide doe eyes. Trishelle registered that the woman's voice was familiar, and that combined with the Santa's Workshop name tag she wore declaring her Ma Freeman meant this woman was the owner of Santa's Workshop, and Big Man, who she now knew by his real name, Jesse, had to be her son and Trishelle's new supervisor.

The embarrassment she'd felt earlier at spitting coffee all over Jesse was nothing compared to waltzing into her new place of employment wrapped in the arms of her half-naked supervisor in front of her new boss, his mother. She had to salvage this somehow. So, she pasted on her best client smile and properly introduced herself.

"Sorry, I should have properly introduced myself the first time. Before our little coffee mishap. I'm Trishelle Harris, or as my followers know me, Holly J. Trishmas." She held out her hand for Jesse to shake, and he looked at her like she'd lost her mind.

"Let me guess, the J stands for Jolly," he said.

She smiled and nodded, but before she could say anything more, he rolled his eyes and turned to his mom.

"I'll grab her a shirt from the back. Call me after you finish all the paperwork," he grumbled before marching away.

Ma Freeman sighed heavily and scowled after her son before turning a bright smile on Trishelle.

"Let's get you started on the paperwork then."

Trishelle nodded and followed Mrs. Freeman to the back office where she filled out the standard new employee paperwork. Jesse didn't return with the shirt but had sent one of his younger siblings to do it. A young boy, who looked almost exactly like Jesse but years younger, burst into the office and haphazardly tossed the shirt at Trishelle.

"Jesse said you needed this," he said before rushing off.

"Please don't judge me by my boy's lack of social training. I swear they get it from their father's side. Now, I am glad you decided to take a chance on coming to work with us. I feel like this could be a great fit for all of us," Mrs. Freeman said.

"Thank You, Mrs. Freeman. I feel the same way, and this opportunity honestly came at the perfect time for me. I really hope it works out the way we both hope," Trishelle said.

"Oh, call me Ma. Everybody else does. And one more thing."

This was the part where Trishelle expected Mrs. Freeman, Ma, to warn her away from her son. To lay out the terms of the fraternization policy. Trishelle would gladly bury her attraction to keep this dream job. What she didn't expect was what actually came out of the woman's mouth.

"Sorry if my Jesse was coming on a bit strong. That boy is a total holiday grinch unless it comes to getting his jollies from the tourists. We don't have a policy against fraternizing since you're the first hire we've had that hasn't been family in one way or the other, but if you do decide to indulge, please make sure it's off the clock," she said.

Trishelle blinked a few times, trying to figure out a proper response to Jesse's mother giving her the green light to fuck her son.

"I promise I can remain professional, regardless of any attraction there may be between me or anyone that may also be employed here at Santa's Workshop," she responded as diplomatically as she could.

Ma took her in for a moment before nodding and straightening the paperwork out on her desk.

"Well then, that is all I have for you here. Jesse is at the front desk with a customer right now, so as soon as you get cleaned up, you can join him to shadow the general tour. The employee changing room is at the end of the hall through the door that says employees only," Ma said.

Dismissed, Trishelle nodded and went to change. The shirt she'd been given was the correct size, and after wiping as much of the sticky dried remnants of coffee as she could from the front of her dress, she slid it on and tied the ends at the waist. It covered the coffee stains and made her dress look more like a fun, festive skirt. She double-checked that her prosthetics were still secure and touched up her makeup before returning to the front.

Jesse, in a new shirt and shorts, stood in front of the large storybook mural that told the origins of Santana and Santa's Workshop. He was already well into the fantastical tale. His eyes twinkled with so much excitement she almost forgot what a grinch he had been earlier. She was captivated by his performance as he made different voices for different characters and even did a silly, prancing move when talking about a reindeer race. She was so engrossed in him and in the tour, she almost forgot she wasn't just a tourist. This was the magic she had come for. The magic she hoped to be able to learn and add to. This was the spirit of Christmas she'd been missing in her old life. When the tour was over, Jesse caught her eye and winked at her, breaking the spell he had woven over her and the crowd.

With a shake of her head, Trishelle knew sleeping with Jesse was inevitable, but that didn't mean she would go so easily to his bed. She had to be sure she wasn't risking her second chance on some wayward lust. So, she made up her mind. Jesse was for flirting only until she'd established herself in town. If things went south between them, she wanted a foundation to ensure she could stick around after. It may be awkward at first, but she just knew Santana was where she was meant to be.

Meet The Reindeer

Jesse

Two days. It had only been two days since Trishelle had waltzed into town and she was already charming the pants off of everyone she met. Like right now, he watched closely as she giggled and grinned at his cousin, Mikey, who nibbled at a carrot in her palm. Trying his best to pretend like he was focused on sweeping up the sawdust-covered puke from a tourist who had one too many at Felix Navidistillery before making their way to Santa's Workshop.

Justin, his little brother, was right beside Mikey, nudging his way in for a chance at being petted and given treats by Trishelle. Their jostling was gentle at first, but Jesse could see it soon getting out of hand. Besides, he didn't like the way Mikey was letting his tongue linger on Trishelle's palm with each nibble.

He tossed the broom aside and marched over to them. He grabbed the decorative reins on his cousin and his brother and pulled them back away from Trishelle. They both stomped and snorted at him but followed his not-so-gentle guidance. He could just see them in their human forms rolling their eyes at him, but for now, they were stuck since they were on duty for back-to-back tours.

"You both need to stop before I swap you out for the twins," he whispered before turning his attention to Trishelle.

She stood in the same spot with her arms crossed over her chest and the cutest little pout on her lips. Today, she wore a glittery green off-the-shoulder number that stopped just above mid-thigh, which was just about where her thigh-high candy cane striped stockings ended. She wore her thick hair in two curly puffs at the sides of her head with a mini elf hat clipped onto the left side.

"I was just bonding with them," she huffed.

"You were being unsafe," he said.

"I was doing exactly what you showed me to do—give them treats with a flat palm and whisper sweet things to them," she said.

Jesse closed the distance between them so he could speak just to her. Shayla was leading the group of tourists through the lobby with the usual parting spiel and he didn't want them, or Shayla for that matter, to hear him reprimanding the adorable little elf.

"The sweet things were for me, not the reindeer, and you forgot rule number one when dealing with wild animals. Don't let them crowd you. You could have gotten hurt if you let them continue carrying on," he said.

Trishelle snorted and shoved playfully at his shoulders. "Then you need to back up, mister."

"What about my sweet things?" he teased.

Trishelle looked around the room before sliding her lithe little body up against his. Her head tipped up, and he couldn't help but bend closer. Her little hand reached up and caressed his cheek before running up and over his ear. He leaned closer, his lips almost touching hers, when he heard the crinkle of a wrapper and suddenly, instead of hot elf lips, his mouth was met with the spicy sweetness of a peppermint candy.

"Sweet enough for you?" She batted her tinsel topped lashes at him, then she giggled and sashayed away.

He crunched on the peppermint as he watched her walk away to join Shayla in greeting the next tour. Behind him, Mikey and Justin huffed and stomped in the reindeer equivalent of a laugh. He shot them both a look over his shoulder before going back to grab the broom and finish cleaning.

Yeah, she was a charmer all right, but Trishelle wasn't yet ready for the kind of reindeer games he had in mind.

Trishelle

She'd almost kissed him. Not even two days on the job and she was already having a hard time keeping her hands off the boss's son. Yes, she was a little peeved that he had interrupted her reindeer bonding time, but the sight of him scowling jealously at the way she cooed and coddled her favorite animal was almost worth it. No one had ever been jealous over her before, at least not so openly, so she'd had no idea it would be such a turn-on.

Her nipples were still hard after being pressed against his warm chest. Those big brown eyes of his had drawn her in. His thick lips had looked so pillowy soft, and dare she say, delicious just seconds from pressing against hers. It was a good thing she'd caught a glimpse of Ma Freeman coming in from the stables, otherwise the tourists arriving for the next tour would have gotten a different kind of show.

It didn't matter that Ma had given her the go-ahead to do whatever with Jesse. Trishelle still needed to stay professional when on the job, and that could only work if she stayed professional outside of it as well. The attraction to him was too strong. She had a hard enough time focusing on work with all the holiday fun Santana had to offer, let alone adding the epitome of a holiday bad boy to the mix.

"Naughty, naughty," Shayla whispered to Trishelle after the tourists were distracted taking pictures with the reindeer.

Shayla was Jesse's sister, and she also helped to run the tours of Santa's Workshop when she wasn't manning the register at the gift shop.

"Not my fault your brother is gorgeous," Trishelle whispered back.

"It does run in the family, but don't let the lure of the grinch get you. Come out with me tonight. There are plenty of eligible bachelors in town that won't turn their nose up at your holiday cheer," Shayla said.

Trishelle was excited about the idea of a night out. She hadn't explored all of Santana yet, since she'd started working almost as soon as she had arrived.

"A night out sounds nice, but I'm honestly not looking. I just got here, and I don't want to accidentally stir up any trouble that would shorten my time here," Trishelle said.

Shayla snorted and waved her hand to signal Jesse to help the tourists wrap things up so they could continue the remainder of the tour.

"Whatever, he's already ensnared you, but tonight, we will dance and be merry and all bah humbuggers be damned," Shayla said.

Trishelle didn't get a chance to ask her to elaborate before the tourists lined up in front of them once more. The Freeman family was certainly full of characters, but Trishelle was quickly realizing that maybe she liked the idea of not being the only weird one in the bunch.

Jesse

The day was finally over, and Jesse's skin itched with the need to shift. He slipped out the back door and headed to the stables. On his way down, he unlocked the doors and let the herd out for the night. Most of the family stayed in reindeer form until they reached their property safely outside the tourist zone, however, some liked to keep a change of clothes in the stables so they could shift as soon as business hours were done. That was why he wasn't surprised at all when Mikey and Justin came running out half-naked while wrestling each other.

"She likes me better!" Justin yelled.

"Nuh-uh, you saw how she lingered to pet me after the shift was over," Mikey boasted.

"She was just consoling you 'cause you almost got puked on by the tourist!" Justin said.

"The tourist only puked because your ass farted in his face. Were you nibbling on turds before shift again?"

"That was one time, and it was your nasty behind that pooped in the trough that morning. Just like you had Jesse trailing poop into the workshop the other day. We need to put you in diapers again until you learn to do your business outside like a good deer," Justin shot back.

Mikey tackled Justin to the ground, and Jesse pinched the bridge of his nose. He was used to Mikey and Justin going at it. The two were either the best of friends or the worst of enemies on any given day. Their teenage hormones were also a factor, meaning the two boys had random partial shifts as they tussled. They were being loud, and the last thing they needed was for Trishelle to overhear their fight and put two and two together sooner than anyone would like. He'd overheard her and Shayla making plans to go out after work, and he knew she would be headed out the back on her way to the walking path that led to the guest trailers.

"Knock it off, you two or I'll kick you out of the running for Santa's Sleigh team this year," Jesse snapped.

The boys stopped rolling around on the ground to stare up at him incredulously. Mikey's face was half deer and Justin's nubby antlers were on full display.

"No way! We worked our butts off last season," Mikey protested.

Jesse put his hands on his hips and glared down at them both.

"You two need to focus on this year. I won't have unruly punks on my team. You made the cut last year to be alternates. If you want to make the team, I need to see some more discipline and less frolicking. You think the tourists want their holiday ruined by flatulent, incontinent, rowdy deer?"

"Are you seriously yelling at the reindeer?" Trishelle's sweet voice floated from just outside the stall where he and the two boys were.

Both of them immediately shifted back to reindeer form, their shorts splitting into rags on the ground as they did so. Thankfully, their transformation was quick, and by the time Trishelle rounded the corner, they were in full reindeer mode, staring dumbly at him.

"What are you doing out here?" Jesse snapped.

She flinched a little but fire danced in her eyes. "I was on my way to change for the night, but I heard voices. I thought maybe some tourists had snuck back here for a private show with the reindeer, but then I heard you yelling at them like a maniac."

Jesse took two deep, calming breaths. He wasn't angry or frustrated with her, and he shouldn't lash out just because she happened to almost catch him and his family in the lie they told the world about the reindeer being well-trained rescues and not human with the ability to shift into reindeer form.

"I'm sorry I snapped at you. Today has been stressful. Everything here is fine. I was just venting," Jesse said.

Trishelle looked from him to the deer before her face softened to one of concern. She slid up next to him, placing her tiny hands on his chest.

"Don't apologize to me. Apologize to them, and the next time you need to vent, can you maybe try journaling, or maybe you can vent to me? I know I'm new here and you don't really know me, but maybe that newness could work in your favor. You know, you can get a third-party perspective on things," she said.

Jesse smirked. "Are you saying you wanna turn my smile upside down? I'm good with that. You know a little six-nine action could be just what I need to blow off some steam," he replied.

Trishelle shook her head before stepping away from him. He felt the loss of her heat like a slab of ice sliding down his back.

"Apologize to the reindeer. They had a rough day too," she said and began to walk away.

"What about turning my smile upside down?" he called after her.

"I think you've had enough of my sweets for one day, don't you?" she called back with a laugh.

Sleigh Ride

Jesse

Santa's Workshop was finally getting a break. For exactly two weeks after Halloween, Santana saw a break in the constant stream of tourists. Enough so that it had become a holiday in its own right for the locals. When they could put down the festive airs and be the quiet town Jesse wished they were every other day of the year. Unfortunately, that break didn't exactly mean there was no work to be done. Although the tours and the photo ops had stopped, this period was used as a time to regroup and revamp their offerings for the new season. It also meant Jesse was in charge of selecting this year's sleigh team while also training Trishelle and somehow keeping her from finding out the real reason that Santa's Workshop cleared of workers whenever it was time for the reindeer to do their thing. So far, she'd happily bought that being wild animals, it was always a good idea to minimize the number of people when they were out and about, despite how well-trained they seemed with crowds.

Just the thought of the perky little elf sent electric heat straight to Jesse's groin. Working with her the last four months had been hell. Not because she wasn't good at her job. No, she was perfect at it. Not only was she good with the customers, but despite being a city girl, she had taken to working in the stables just fine. The young reindeer loved being featured in her social media content. She was able to get them to do things even he couldn't convince them to do. Sometimes, a little too well. In the last video, they'd done a version of the can-can in reindeer form and the comments had been concerning. People speculated that they weren't real animals but humans in costume, that they were animatronics, or even some said it had been manipulated with editing. It had brought enough scrutiny that people had started to speculate about other things around Santana, and that wasn't good for business.

It was on his to-do list to ask her to tone it down a bit with the content. Something he knew wasn't going to go over well with her and make it even harder for him to get her to drop whatever Teflon shield she had up against the attraction he knew she had for him. Yeah, that's why her being there was hell because every day he watched her sexy little ass strut around in her barely family-friendly costumes. Every day he dealt with her sweet smiles and that adorable little nose wiggle wink thing she did for her followers online and the new fans she made out of the tourists. Worse, even though she laughed off any attempt he made to get her alone for a private show, she still flirted.

Like now, even as she put on a show in front of the camera, she flipped her frilly green tutu up just enough to flash him a peek at her white panties decorated with little holly berries. A completely unnecessary move when the camera was only capturing her from the waist up. He knew the move was for him because not only was he the only other person in the small area they had sectioned off to be her filming space, but also because she looked directly at him and not the camera when she winked.

"Alright, my Little Jollies! That was it for today's Candy Cane twist tutorial! Be sure to tune in next week to watch me take the reins on Santa's Sleigh! Have a Holly Jolly Trishmas!" She wiggled her nose and winked again, this time to the camera before ending her live. Then she moved to the small speaker and cut off her remixed version of I Wish It Could Be Christmas Everyday by Wizzard.

"And who gave you permission to do that?" he asked, forcing himself to sound perturbed instead of turned on by the thought of her with a pair of leather reins in her hand. Especially considering he'd be one of the reindeer she'd be using them on, even if she didn't know it.

Trishelle spun around and sidled right up to him, invading his personal space, and even though he had to tilt his head almost to his chin to meet her gaze, he knew she was in charge. She could ask him anything as long as her hot little body was pressed against his and he'd cave like his last and only attempt at making a chocolate souffle. A fact she clearly knew as she batted her long eyelashes over the honey brown of her eyes. The fake frosted tips brushed the tops of her silver glitter-dusted cheeks.

She'd gone for what he'd heard her call her frosted sugar plum look. The general tones were silvery and sparkly, like fresh snow had fallen and just barely melted across her eyelids and cheeks. The tip of her nose was dusted with an icy pink blush, but it was her lips that were the brain killer. Outlined with a deep red that blended into a soft-looking peach before she finished it with a thick shimmering lip gloss that made them look like juicy fruit he would love to dive into and get lost in.

"You did, don't you remember?" she asked huskily.

He shook his head, "Actually I don't."

Honestly, he was pretty sure it had never come up in conversation because no one got to hold the reins other than him, his Pa, and whoever played Santa that year. A standing rule because not only were reindeer wild animals, but these particular wild animals were also shifters and all it would take was one tap of the reins that was a little too rough for all hell to break loose. Everyone knew that, including Trishelle, because it was one of the first rules given when starting as a new hire. You had to work up to the privilege to even ride the sleigh, let alone drive it, and while she had done an amazing job so far, a few months on the job was not long enough to earn that privilege.

"You sure you don't remember?" She ran her palms up his chest. Her nails applied just enough pressure to give him an idea of how they would feel scraping against his bare flesh if he ever got the chance to make good on all the flirting they'd done the last few months.

Fuck! The way she stared up at him expectantly, a glitter of promise in her eyes if he would fold to her whims. Maybe he wasn't so far gone just yet, because normally he would give her anything in a moment like this. One thing he couldn't and wouldn't budge on was the rules about the sleigh. Especially considering how dangerous it was for everyone involved.

He covered her hands with his, bringing them together over his heart before drawing them up to his lips and pressing a gentle kiss across her knuckles. "Sorry, sweetheart, you know the rules. No one drives the sleigh but me, Pa, or whoever plays this year's Santa."

She pouted and pulled her hands and body out of his reach. "Are you sure?"

"I can't let you drive the sleigh, but I can give you a ride once the team is selected and trained," he offered.

He could see the exact moment she realized further pleading wasn't going to work; her shoulders slumped, and she sighed.

"Ugh, now I owe your sister fifty bucks," she muttered.

From a dark corner of the room, his sister Shayla ugly chortled, "I told you no amount of honey would get you on that sleigh!"

His arousal quickly turned to anger and embarrassment. He'd known Trishelle and his little sister had gotten close, but to have his emotions played with, and for a bet at that. No, now they both would have to pay. Trishelle technically would have been trained with the sleigh anyway because as Santa's main helper, she would have been assigned the task of tossing treats from the goodie bag during the parade and later handing out little gifts to the children who came to sit on Santa's lap. Now however, he would ensure she never set foot on the sleigh. As for his sister? Well, he had other ways of dealing with her.

"Uh oh! We've pissed off the grinch," Shayla laughed harder.

Trishelle hung her head like she was ashamed but he saw the way her shoulders bounced with her laughter, even in the still dim lighting. He didn't have to put up with this. He started to march out of the room, almost forgetting he had come to talk to her about her crazy reindeer stunts online. He spun back around, a smug smile on his face.

"Laugh it up, chuckles. Keep that up while you have to figure out your content for the next month without the help of the reindeer. Oh, and Shayla? You're on muck duty for twice that."

With that, he spun on his heels and skipped out of the room. Yes, skipped, because while he was admittedly not a fan of the year-round holiday cheer, that didn't mean he had a permanent stick up his butt. No matter what his family and the rest of the town thought.

Trishelle

Was it bad that she was too busy watching Jesse's ass as he skipped away from her that it took her a few minutes too long to realize he'd just ruined her carefully crafted social media plan with one edict? Could she still make content without the reindeer? Yes. That was evidenced in the fact her latest video not featuring them had done just as well. To be fair, she knew it had nothing to do with her flirtatious stunt, but most likely because the comment section had turned into a brutal debate on whether it was real or not.

If Trishelle hadn't seen it happen live, she wouldn't have believed it was real either. She'd only been joking when she'd said she wanted the reindeer to attempt the can-can. Jesse had only just taught her the basic commands to get the reindeer to do more than just stand there looking adorable. Yet when she'd given the command to kick, they'd started right up, and thankfully, she'd already had the camera running.

From there, she had hoped to do more with the reindeer kick-line, but now she'd have to go back to the drawing board. Not only that, she would have to pull on her head elf panties to face Jesse and apologize. Before he'd gotten pissed, she'd seen the flicker of hurt in his eyes. She'd gone too far trying to use their mutual attraction for her gain, but by the time she attempted to catch up with him he was already disappearing into the dark tree line of the forest.

"Hey! Don't worry about it. Give him a minute to chill out and he'll reinstate your privileges asap," Shayla said coming up behind her.

"No, I need to address this now," she said and took off after him.

She could see the trail decently enough but as she reached the tree line herself, Jesse was nowhere to be found. Instead, in the middle of the path stood a giant buck, his large antlers almost as wide as the well-traveled path.

She stalled out. While she did fine with the more domesticated reindeer at the workshop, the wild reindeer the farm sheltered and allowed to roam the forest freely were another thing altogether. She stood frozen as it made eye contact with her. She tried hard to remember what Jesse had said to do when encountering one of the wild reindeer, but all thought escaped her when it started to walk in her direction. She stood frozen as it approached, trying to stay as calm as possible monitoring her breathing. Should she look away? Yeah, she should probably look away, but she just couldn't. She was stuck, captivated, intrigued, and scared out of her mind. It was even bigger up close, especially as it invaded her space.

Was this how she was going to die? She could see the headlines now. *Holiday influencer not so jolly after reindeer can-canned her head in.* Well, surely, they would come up with something much more comical and concise but yeah, she was surely going to die. She closed her eyes; she could feel hot breath on her face and then the unthinkable happened. It nudged her. Not roughly, but enough to get her to stumble backward. She was still frozen in place when it nudged her again. Her eyes flew open, and it tilted its head to the side before nodding toward the forest edge. Was it telling her to git or was it just playing with her before she was attacked? When it nodded and stomped its foot at her, she figured it was probably the latter, but hey, if she could make it out of the forest someone would see and be able to help her. So, she turned and ran like her life depended on it.

When she emerged from the forest, she nearly ran over Shayla who stood there with amusement glinting in her eyes.

"Oh my god! I'm being chased!" Trishelle screamed, jumping onto Shayla.

"Calm down, girl! That's just Jay! He's harmless. Mostly."

"Jay?" Trishelle recognized the name of one of the domesticated bucks Shayla had introduced her to. She'd told her the buck was Jesse's pet, but Trishelle had never seen the two of them together before.

"Yeah, come on. You look like you need a drink and Feliz Navidistillery is having their new cocktail contest tonight," Shayla said and pulled Trishelle away from the forest.

Trishelle took one last look back, but the trail was clear, both Jay and Jesse nowhere in sight. She took a deep breath and decided it was probably best she listened to her friend. No use getting herself killed trying to chase him down in the unfamiliar forest. They would have to chat later.

Feliz Navidistillery had a small bar on Main Street that offered only a fraction of their full menu, but the main distillery was on the edge of town just past Nightmare on 34th Street, the Halloween-themed block of Santana. Trishelle had admittedly steered clear of the area in the months she had been living and working in Santana. The town wasn't very big, but every day Main Street had been filled with new faces and attractions that had kept her occupied outside of work when she wasn't so tired that she just crashed in her trailer. One of the six kept on the Freeman Reindeer Rescue that were usually rented out to other seasonal employees around town.

She hadn't ventured farther than Main Street until about a week ago when Shayla had insisted they finally go out for that drink she'd promised the first week on the job. Feliz Navidistillery was already bustling with locals despite the relatively early hour.

"I told you this week was when we locals get to let our hair down a bit. Don't be surprised by anything you see tonight," Shayla said with a wink before pulling them both to the bar.

Jesus was behind the bar. His family, the Felicidades, owned the distillery and handled the nativity scene in the town square. He was a couple years older than her and Shayla, but Shayla acted as if he were at least ten years their senior. Initially, Trishelle had thought it was playful teasing because his long hair was bleached to a shocking platinum blonde. Though now, she was pretty sure it was a defense mechanism against the obvious attraction between the two of them, much like Trishelle joined in on Jesse's family pranks to keep him at arm's length.

"'Sup, gramps, slide me two of those Yuletide Flamers," Shayla said, hopping up onto the bar. Not sitting on one of the stools readily available, but parking her jean-clad ass right on the bar top.

Jesus rolled his eyes as he grabbed Shayla by the waist and slid her off the bar and into his arms. "Now, now, Shay Baby, how many times have I told you not to get on my bar like that? Do I need to take you over my knee and teach you the hard way?"

Shayla giggled and batted her eyelashes before wiggling out of his grasp. "Show me how to make one and I promise not to for a whole month."

"Sugar plum, you know I don't share my recipes, but I'll make yours extra special."

"Ooh, pinky promise?" Shayla said, holding out her pinky to him.

Instead of looping his pinky with hers, he bent down and sucked it into his mouth and suckled for a second before pulling away with an audible pop.

"Get your sexy ass from behind my bar before my pinky makes a promise you won't let me keep," he laughed.

Shayla giggled more and made a show of sucking that same pinky into her mouth as she sauntered out from behind the bar. Jesus made their drinks while keeping his eye on Shayla, and by the time Shayla made her way back around to Trishelle, he slid the flaming shooters across the bar.

"You two should just fuck already and put everyone in town out of their misery of watching your little reindeer games," a gruff voice said from behind them.

Jesus looked pissed, and Shayla suddenly became a less confident flirt and more guilty like a toddler. Trishelle thought maybe one of Shayla's large family had made the comment, but when she turned around, she saw it was one of Marguerite's sons.

"Terry," Shayla said softly.

"Nah, nope. I'm not doing this with you two today. You told me you chose him, and yet, I don't see him treating you half as good as I was. Hell, he's too chicken shit to actually claim you for real, so miss me with your pity, and Jesus, do your job and grab me a draft. Keep that glare for some dumb fuck who doesn't know you couldn't fight your way out of a paper bag if your life depended on it."

Trishelle stood stunned at the drama unfolding before her. She'd known Shayla was banned from the coffeehouse but no one had told her why. She never would have guessed it was because Shayla had apparently broken the heart of one of the fabled Wee Bear brothers.

"Man, come on. Don't get us banned from the only place to get a decent drink in miles," Carey, the taller of the three brothers said, pushing forward from the crowd.

He chatted amicably with Jesus as Shayla downed her drink with little fanfare before grabbing Trishelle and pulling her to the cleared-out space that served as a makeshift dance floor where the patrons were line dancing to *Rockin' Around the Christmas Tree*. Trishelle opened her mouth to ask Shayla about Terry, but Shayla shot her a look and did a twirl, putting a person between them. A clear sign she wasn't ready to talk about it just then, maybe not ever. Trishelle reminded herself that although they had gotten close, it had only been recently. So, she dropped it and focused on learning the steps to the dance. Maybe if she learned it well enough, she could use it for content to replace the reindeer content she was losing out on.

Jesse

Watching Trishelle twirl around on the dance floor at Feliz Navidistillery had not been on his to-do list for the evening. He should have been up at his cabin using his newfound free time to finish the renovations necessary for him to live there full time. He only had a month left before the cold and snow would put a halt to his progress, and he was already behind schedule. Still, he'd needed to make sure she was okay after he'd scared the living daylights out of her. If he hadn't been so pissed off, he would have heard her following him into the woods. He wouldn't have shifted to his reindeer so close to the trail where she had caught him. Thankfully, he'd tucked his clothes away around the bend in the trail where she couldn't see.

She seemed totally fine now, but he hadn't been able to leave. Not just because she was captivating as she shimmied, stomped, and twirled around with his sister, but because he wasn't the only man who had noticed. Santana in the off times was hard up for young single women not related to you, and Trishelle was fresh meat. He hadn't wanted to confuse people by staking a claim on her, knowing she was here possibly temporarily and she wasn't in the know. Unlike other supernaturals in the area, he had some ground rules when it came to naïve humans. He would take a tumble in the hay with any that were willing, but what he would never do was claim or mark one who had no idea what that even meant.

Hell, all he and Trishelle had was a flirtation at this point and some aggravating teasing. Nothing to hold any of the less scrupulous at bay, so yeah, he sat there and watched to make sure he could swoop in and warn off any who tried. He didn't even have to say he was interested in her; he could play it off as protecting his family's employee. At least, that is what he told himself when he saw Carey closing in. He knew he had no chance if the bear was looking for a fight, plus there was the unfortunate situation with Shayla and Carey's brother Terry who had almost gotten the whole Freeman clan banned from the coffeehouse. A fight with Carey would likely tip the scales in that regard, no matter how much Marguerite loved him.

Still, his fate was sealed the moment Carey looked up and winked at him before sliding his grimy little paw around Trishelle's waist. Jesse hadn't even realized he'd moved until he was snatching Trishelle away from the man like a rag doll.

"Hands off, buddy," he said just a little too harshly.

Carey had the nerve to laugh and raise his hands. "All right, Rudolph, Ma warned me you'd staked your claim, but when I didn't see you parading her around, I thought she was free game," he said as if to explain.

Jesse shook his head. "She's vegetarian, it would never work out for ya either way."

"I'm not," Trishelle started but shut her mouth as Jesse tightened his grip on her in warning.

Carey nodded and walked away. As soon as he was out of sight, Jesse nodded at Shayla before dragging Trishelle out of the bar. He'd wanted to give her space, keep her at arm's length for her sake, but now. Now he was done with all of that. She'd played with him too much not to accept the consequences, even if that meant all he got was a slap in the face and a vacancy for head elf. Once outside, he pushed Trishelle up against the wall and kissed her. She tensed at first before moaning and joining in, her lips parting and her little tongue darting out to duel with his. If she'd surrendered to their attraction sooner, he may have been able to control himself better. He would have taken his time to savor the taste of her hot little mouth, let his hands roam over all her curves and valleys, tease out all the little spots that made her swoon and squeal in delight, but not now. Not with the jealousy riding him hard, the many days and nights left wanting her. Still, if she pushed him away, if she gave him any indication that he'd made all of this sexual attraction up in his head, he would stop. He would let her go back to the bar with Shayla, or if she let him after he made such an ass of himself, he'd walk her to her trailer and never bother her again. He knew that, but he needed her to know it too.

"Trish, love, tell me to stop and I will. Tell me you don't want this, want me, and I'll let this go," he breathed between the kisses he trailed down her neck.

Her response was to hop up and wrap her legs around his waist, grinding her sweet center against his belt buckle. "If you stop right now, I'll never speak to you again," she gasped.

That was all he needed. It didn't matter that they were by no means hidden just a few feet from the main entrance to the distillery, but at this time of night everyone who wanted to be there was already inside and anyone stumbling out this early would probably be on the same kind of time or too drunk to notice or care. He fumbled with his buckle to free himself, desperate to feel her heat on his length, but he had the presence of mind to fish a condom out of his wallet with one hand while the other sampled the depths of her slick heat.

"Jesse, please!" she begged as she rode his hand.

Apparently, his fingers weren't enough for her either. Fingers he reluctantly withdrew so he could make sure he was properly wrapped before he sank into her treasure. He let out a low groan as he struggled not to cum like an inexperienced schoolboy as her tight little channel gripped every inch of his length as he slid in. On a whim, he began to sing Oh Holy Night as he slid in and out of her heat. A desperate attempt to keep himself from embarrassing himself by finishing before she did. It worked, sort of. He made it to the first chorus before losing the battle with his body, the last note coming out a strangled cry of release. At least he wasn't alone when he came. His strangled groan was drowned out with Trishelle's beautiful high note as her inner muscles clenched and released rapidly around his cock, milking him and prolonging his release.

Then there was nothing but the muffled sound of the music thumping inside and their harsh sawing breaths as they came down from the high. Then Trishelle started laughing, "I definitely have splinters in my ass."

Jesse pushed back to look her in the eyes. "Really?"

"What, am I supposed to not tell you about the ass splinters you gave me? You definitely owe me a sleigh ride now."

She smiled and made jokes when all Jesse wanted was to declare his ruin. She'd ruined him for other women. While he'd suspected his attraction to her was something more, he hadn't known until he had her that he was never letting her go.

"Sorry, sweetheart, but the only thing you're riding is me," he breathed.

You're A Mean One, Mr. Grinch

Trishelle

Her ass stung with splinters, her legs felt like Jello, and the only thing keeping her up was Jesse's heavy body leaning against her, pressing her back into the wood of the converted barn that housed the distillery. She could feel the music from inside vibrating against her back just as surely as she could feel Jesse's heart racing in his chest pressed against hers.

She'd joked with him about the sleigh ride to cut the intense moment between them. To halt the train of thought her mind had been on as she'd orgasmed harder than she ever had in her entire life. Someone singing one of the OG Christmas songs while screwing her brains out where anyone could walk by and see was a new kink unlocked.

The problem was she wasn't sure it would be a turn-on with anyone but Jesse.

Their prolonged flirtation may have had a hand in the explosiveness of this encounter but something deep inside was telling her it was something more. Trishelle had always been practical when it came to relationships. She'd always been able to walk away from flings unscathed. She'd even been able to walk away from her last relationship of five years with only a day or two of feeling crappy about it. Yet she knew if Jesse turned out to be the playboy everyone in town claimed he was and this night was all there was? She wasn't sure she'd be able to recover so easily.

"There won't be any more riding anything if I don't get these splinters out my ass," she breathed.

While that was true, she also needed some space. She didn't want to have post-coital cuddles clouding her decision to keep things light with Jesse. He groaned and ground into her one last time before disconnecting their lower halves. When he'd finished tucking himself back into his pants, she thought he would finally let her get back on her feet but instead, he wrapped his arms tighter around her waist and started carrying her down the street.

"Jesse! What are you doing? Put me down!"

"And watch you limp your splintered ass back to the workshop? What kind of shit boyfriend do you think I am?"

She tensed. "Boyfriend? Really?"

"What? You don't want me? Not into labels? Too bad, should have thought of that before you screamed my name so loud the whole town knows your ass belongs to me."

"How are you so certain they even heard over that screeching, albeit inspired, rendition of Oh Holy Night?" she shot back.

"Oh, they heard, and I'll have you know I have the voice of an angel. That shrieking was all you, love," he said and pinched her ass.

"Ouch! Put me down, asshole!"

"So, we've graduated to name-calling? After I help you with your splinter situation, I might just bend you over my knee," he chuckled.

"What? Who asked you for help, and don't you dare try to spank me! I'm a grown-ass woman with no interest in daddy kink," she huffed.

"Did I say anything about being your daddy? No, I believe I said boyfriend, and we both know Santa's your real fantasy. Yeah, I can just see you all trussed up in that sexy little green velvet number you wore on your first day in town. That tiny skirt barely covering your ass as you work Santa's candy cane and he tells you what a good little elf you are."

She glared at him, not because he was wrong, but because he was exactly right about that being one of her fantasies.

"Don't tell me it's not true. I can feel how wet you are right now," he said, his thumb running along her slit, forcing her to tighten her legs and lean more into his grasp.

"Fuck you," she breathed.

"Exactly. Remember who this pussy belongs to. You can fantasize about being a good little elf for old-ass Santa if you want to, but the reality is you aren't a good elf, Trishelle. No, you're far too naughty. You know what Santa does to naughty little elves?"

"No, but I know you plan to enlighten me," she breathed.

Her traitorous body had her wiggling her hips to get his thumb to stop tracing the edges of her panty line and making contact with her sensitive nub. Her splinters were long forgotten as she desperately chased the orgasm his teasing fingers kept just out of reach.

He leaned in and nibbled on her earlobe before whispering, "He feeds them to his reindeer."

She started to laugh, but it turned into a strangled, "Oh god!" as his thumb pressed firmly on her clit, and with one circular movement, a second orgasm tore through her.

"Not God either, love. Jesse, your boyfriend. Now let's get those splinters taken care of so we can get back to having fun."

Trishelle blinked a few times as he cut on some lights. She'd been so caught up in their conversation and her arousal that she hadn't realized they were now inside. Not her trailer or the workshop, but what looked like a partially renovated cabin.

"What is this place?" she asked.

"My home, at least, it will be once I get it all finished." He carried her down a short hallway and nudged open a door at the end of the hall.

The room they entered was sparse, just a bed and a dresser, but it was clean and neat. Jesse eased her gently onto the bed.

"I'll be right back," he said and disappeared out the door.

Shaking her head, Trishelle wondered how she'd gotten so caught up so fast, but she knew why. This was what happened when you held out on your cravings. Either they went away by the time you got to indulge and weren't as satisfying, or like in this case, it was even better than imagined and you ran the risk of overindulging to the point you couldn't stomach the craving any longer.

Trishelle was afraid she was well on the path of overindulgence but there was no one to stop her and remind her that moderation was key. Jesse sure as hell wasn't going to be that person. He was already labeling them a couple. She had no idea what that even meant for him, and she knew she needed to ask before she agreed to anything further.

Jesse came back into the room with a bottle of white glue and some rubbing alcohol in his hands.

"Turn over, ass up," he demanded with a smirk on his face.

"What kind of prank are you trying to pull now, Jesse?"

"No prank, I've had plenty of splinters in my life, and white glue is the best way to get them out without spending hours with a pair of tweezers and a magnifying glass."

"I don't believe you."

"Trust me," he pressed.

Trishelle bit her lip before doing as he asked.

"You better not glue my ass cheeks together or some nonsense," she muttered into his comforter.

He snorted. "I should with the way you've been teasing me these past couple of months, but no, I've got other plans for that ass that require full access."

Before she could ask what kind of plans, she felt him drizzle the cold glue on her cheeks over the stinging splinters. The cool glue felt a little too good on her irritated skin, especially as he gently spread it with his fingers.

"Next time, it will be ropes of my cum decorating your ass. Would you let me do that, Trishelle? Would you like me to fuck you into a quivering mess before decorating your pretty ass like an abstract art piece?"

"Why are you so nasty? You barely talk to me unless it's to say some off-the-wall dirty shit," she said.

Her back arched as he blew gently on the wet glue.

"I only say what I mean, that's why. From the moment I saw you tear into that punk ass tourist, I've wanted to be buried balls deep in you, and I could see in your eyes you would have let me too if we hadn't found out we would be working together. I get you trying to keep things professional to a certain extent, but I'm not in the habit of denying myself the things I want. That being said, if you don't like me telling you exactly what's on my mind whenever I see you, I can reel it in."

"So, you are serious about this whole boyfriend thing?"

She tried to focus on anything but him blowing on her ass and how it was making her wet all over again.

"As a heart attack. You're mine, Trishelle. Exclusively if that wasn't already implied."

"Just because we had sex doesn't mean we have to..." The words died in her mouth as he began to slowly peel the now dry glue off her ass and followed with soft kisses to her sensitive flesh.

"No, it doesn't, but I'm telling you that's what I want. What is it that you want, Trishelle? You can tell me, I'm a big boy. Are you going to be my naughty little elf and let this reindeer eat you up to his heart's content?" He nipped gently at her inner thigh.

Trishelle took a minute to think about it. To ignore the heat racing through her, the arousal pooling between her legs, the gentle nuzzling and licking everywhere but her core. She couldn't lie about wanting Jesse, wanting to explore the attraction to him, but she wasn't sure she felt comfortable labeling him her boyfriend when so far, they'd only been teasing coworkers.

"You say you want to be my boyfriend, but you've done nothing to earn the title. I'll be your naughty little elf, but you've gotta take me on a date or two before I feel comfortable making this official," she said.

"Done," Jesse said without hesitation before diving between her legs.

He gripped the back of her thighs and pulled her down over his mouth. Trishelle gripped the sheets and buried her face into the mattress to muffle her screams as he made good on his promise to eat her to his heart's content.

Jesse

Jesse grinned to himself as he held Trishelle's sleeping body close to his. Last night had been amazing. Once he'd agreed to her stipulations about dates, she'd shown him just how naughty she could be. It had been well into the early hours of the morning before they'd finally collapsed together and fallen asleep. If it wasn't for years of waking up before the crack of dawn, Jesse would still be asleep too.

Instead, he lay there reveling in the feeling of her next to him and making plans on how to woo Trishelle into being comfortable with his claim on her. The first step, be boyfriend material. Second, get the balls to tell her he was a reindeer shifter, and if she didn't freak the fuck out and try to get him committed or worse, locked up in a lab somewhere, he would ask her to be his forever mate.

Baby steps. Which meant planning a couple of dates around town was first on the list. He wasn't sure he wanted to let her go back to her trailer anytime soon, but he also knew the more she was around, the less likely he could keep the secret of being a shifter from her. Speaking of, he should probably let himself run a bit before she woke up. He'd been staying in his human form more than usual with her in town and his animal half wasn't exactly a fan.

Carefully, he slipped out of bed and headed outside. It didn't matter that he was naked, he'd ruin any clothes he had on anyway in his shift. He ran free for about an hour before heading into town to grab some coffee and breakfast for himself and Trishelle. His kitchen might be functional, but his fridge was damn near bare. After the night they'd shared, Trishelle would undoubtedly be starving and probably wouldn't appreciate a smoothie of assorted grasses and oats as was his usual breakfast fare.

Trishelle might not be a vegetarian, but he was, despite all the talk he did about reindeer eating elves. Although, he'd quite enjoyed feasting on her multiple times last night. He ignored the knowing look from Valerie at the town market as she rang up his packet of bacon, a carton of eggs, and a box of pancake mix. Not part of his usual grocery run, for sure, and he didn't make a habit of cooking for his tourist flings. Jesse was pretty sure the rumor mill would be buzzing within the hour about him shacking up with Trishelle.

He just hoped the gossip wouldn't reach Trishelle's ears before the worst of it had been dropped in favor of a juicier story. No doubt there would be some talk of her being just the flavor of the month or some other bullshit, but that wasn't what he was about. At least, not with Trishelle. At the same time, he didn't want them spilling the whole fated mate tea early either. He knew that would definitely send Trishelle running for the hills, or rather, back to the city.

He paid for the groceries and headed to Jingle Bell Java to grab their coffees. Despite his order from the day they met, Jesse was more of a no-frills black coffee kind of guy. He'd learned that while she did occasionally splurge on a creamer-laden sugar bomb, Trishelle's preferred daily cup was simple. Two shots of espresso with one pump of peppermint and two pumps of chocolate syrup. Proof she could in fact handle holiday flare in moderation. Marguerite served up both with a smile and a wink and then he was on his way back to set up the rest of their day.

Jesse was strolling through the workshop whistling a happy tune as he tackled the daily chores early when he stumbled across Shayla who looked like her night had ended on a far less happy note.

"Hey, sis! What's going on?" he asked.

She raised her head from the front desk, her eyes red and her cheeks streaked with tears.

"I made a mistake," she wailed before continuing to sob.

Jesse had no idea when Trishelle was going to wake up, and the last thing he wanted was for her to find him gone when she did. Yet, he was a big brother first, and seeing Shayla in tears like this hadn't happened since she was twelve and learned that Santa wasn't real. How it took that long was a mystery to him, but that didn't matter right now. He made his way around the desk and pulled his sister into a hug. He rubbed her back as she sobbed into his chest. When it seemed she had quieted enough to talk, he asked more questions.

"Is this a mistake something I can help with?"

She shook her head.

"Is it boy-related?"

She nodded her head.

"I'm going to assume this mistake involves a certain Fae bartender since Marguerite wasn't slamming the door in my face this morning."

She nodded again.

"Do I finally get to kick his smug little ass?"

She shook her head.

"Are you sure? Like one hundred percent sure, because I'll do it, no further questions asked. Just say the word and he'll get a reindeer stomping he'll never forget."

She snorted out a laugh between sobs before pulling away.

"I'm pregnant," she whispered.

It took a moment for her words to fully register.

"Oh. Oh! Geez, Shayla, and that asshole was serving you alcohol? You were drinking last night!" Now he was angry with her.

"He was serving me mocktails all night, but that's not the mistake part."

"Okay? Did he finally get over himself and claim you? I mean, other than just physically, obviously."

"We don't know the baby is his. I know the town thinks I chose Jesus over Terry, and I did, but I kinda regretted it, so I was seeing them both again, privately, of course. That's why Jesus hasn't claimed me. He knows my heart is torn between the two of them and while he's open to sharing, Terry isn't because he's too afraid to admit he kinda has a thing for Jesus too."

Jesse took a step back. "Whoa, whoa, I'm going to stop you right there. You telling me Jesus and Terry also," he made the finger-hole penetration movement with his hands and Shayla rolled her eyes.

"Grow up, Jesse. Yes, Terry is fluid, at least when it comes to me and Jesus. He just doesn't want the whole town gossiping about it and us, but now? With this baby?"

Jesse ran his hand over his face before whistling. "Yet, you just blabbed to me about it."

"Only because I know you wouldn't judge, and you don't take part in the rumor mill, and you caught me at a vulnerable moment," she was rambling.

Shayla only rambled when things were really bothering her. Jesse pulled her back into a hug. "Your secret is safe with me, and it doesn't matter if your kid comes out a cub, calf, or a goddamned Fae. I'll give them just as much shit as I do the rest of the children in Santana," he promised.

She snorted another laugh. "Thank you, and also don't tell Ma just yet. She's already suspicious, but I want to announce it at Thanksgiving. Hopefully, by then, we'll know."

"Yeah, if your belly is as big as a Mac truck, we know it's Terry, and if we still can't tell even though you're how far along?"

"By Thanksgiving, 8 months," she said.

"Fuck, it's a Fae. You are breeding another emotional terrorist if you're not already showing."

"Oh, I'm showing, but Jesus has used glamour to help me hide it."

"Next, you'll be telling me your due date is Christmas and you're naming them something tragically Christmas specific..." He stopped when he saw her grin.

"Jesus and Terry both like North Star, and it's gender neutral," she replied.

"Even I can't hate that name," he chuckled.

"Good, though, I wouldn't give a shit either way, you big grinch."

Now that he'd put a smile back on his sister's face, Jesse needed to get a move on. The sun was already up, and that meant Trishelle surely would be too. He didn't exactly have window coverings at the cabin.

"Glad I could help, but I gotta run," he said.

"Right, you finally scored with Trishelle and officially ruined my favorite Christmas song."

"Does that mean I won't have to hear it twelve times a day? You're welcome." He grinned while picking up his discarded groceries and coffees and walking backward toward the door. "I'm headed back to my lady love now to hopefully ruin more of your Christmas faves."

"Eww, just don't fuck things up with my new best friend. Don't let her be blindsided by the deer shifter news if you're serious about her."

"You mean, don't complete our mating bond before she knows I magically shapeshift into her favorite Christmas animal, or make sure I tell her before she figures it out on her own and runs back to the city?"

"Exactly," Shayla said with a wink and a wave of her hand.

"That's not happening," Trishelle's sweet voice said from behind him.

Jesse nearly dropped the coffees as he whirled around to face her. She stood in the doorway wearing yesterday's clothes with her arms were crossed over her chest. Jesse hadn't known how good of a poker face Trishelle had, but he definitely could not tell what was going on in her head other than she was pissed.

Trishelle

She shouldn't have been eavesdropping. She hadn't meant to. She had woken up to an empty bed and figured Jesse hadn't meant what he said to her last night about wanting to explore things with her outside the bedroom. Then, she decided instead of moping about it that she would head into the workshop early to figure out her new plan for content without the reindeer.

She'd gotten to the workshop before even thinking about the fact that she was in last night's clothes because her head was elsewhere. She'd been just about to turn around and head to her trailer to change when she'd heard Shayla sobbing.

Being a good friend, she went to investigate, only to find Jesse already there consoling her. It was sweet, and she hadn't been able to resist the temptation of seeing the softer side of Jesse. Then their conversation had taken a wild turn to Fae and bears, and then...

Yeah, she'd read enough Gen Ursa novels to know what a shifter was and what a mate bond meant, at least in theory. Applied to real life, she wasn't sure. Applied to her life? Get the fuck out, but also, she couldn't discount that Jesse and Shayla had caught her snooping and were playing another one of their pranks. If there was one thing

Trishelle had learned about the Freeman clan, it was that a prank could be extremely simple or extremely elaborate, and Jesse had promised to get her back for the bet she'd made with Shayla yesterday.

She decided that was it. That this was an attempt at a prank, and she could play along too.

"Trishelle! Uh, how much of that did you hear, and um, which part isn't happening?" Jesse looked terrified, but she knew he was a good actor too, so she stuck with her plan.

"Enough to know Shayla is pregnant, congratulations by the way, and that you think I'll run back to the city after finding out you're a shifter. Which I won't and I'm not. If you're serious about the whole mate bond thing, I'm down to explore it," she said with as straight of a face as she could manage.

Jesse stared at her as if she had two heads. "You sure about that? You seem a little too calm about all of this."

"Try me," she shrugged.

She had no idea what that meant, but the last thing she expected was for Jesse to slowly turn to look at his sister before setting the things he carried on the front desk and beginning to strip naked.

"All right, you asked for it," he said and as soon as he was naked his body began to contort unnaturally, a tawny pelt sprouted from his skin, and within seconds, Jesse was no longer in front of her but a giant buck that looked suspiciously like Jay.

Her mouth dropped open. This was so not a prank. She shrieked and backed into the wall. "Oh my god, this isn't a prank! I thought this was payback for yesterday, but you're seriously fucking for real right now!"

"Uh, yeah, this is real. I'd shift too, but I can't because you know, baby. Anyway, I'll leave my dumbass brother to handle the rest of the explaining. I do hope you decide to stay, or at the very least, not tell the world if you do decide to go. See you later, bestie!" Shayla said and walked out, leaving Trishelle alone with a giant fucking reindeer in the middle of Santa's Workshop.

She expected Jesse to shift back once his sister was gone, but he stayed as a deer and approached her slowly, just like he had in the forest. Only this time when he nuzzled her, it was gently, almost a plea. Cautiously, Trishelle reached up to pet his neck.

"It's really you in there, right, Jesse? Or are you not quite there when in animal form?"

Jay snorted in response and nudged her again. She assumed that meant Jesse was very much present as an animal. She continued to pet its neck, the action was calming and helped her concentrate on the most important of her questions.

"So, all that talk about Santa feeding me to his reindeer was your way of hinting at this?"

Jay nodded his head.

"And everyone who works here is a shifter but me?"

Jay snorted, so she assumed that was a no.

"But most of them are? Most of the people in this town are?"

Jay nodded.

Trishelle took a deep breath and let it out slowly. It was a lot to take in; she was having a hard time adjusting to having an actual conversation with a deer.

"Can you shift back now? I want to talk with Jesse."

Jay took a couple of steps back before crouching and shifting back. The transition back to human form was almost worse to watch than the transition from human to animal. When Jesse slowly unfurled to his full height, Trishelle forced herself not to look at his dick and to focus on his face. She'd felt how big it was last night, but she hadn't taken the time to see how big it was. She bit her lip and focused squarely on his face. Jesse smirked and shook his head.

"Yeah, all of that was inside you last night, and hopefully again real soon, if you're good with that," he said.

She shouldn't be good with that, but she kinda was. Naked Jesse was stunning, and it made it easy to almost forget that he'd been a giant fucking reindeer half a minute prior.

"Can you put clothes on?"

"Sure thing." Jesse slid his clothes on before grabbing the two coffee cups he'd discarded earlier and closing the distance between them. Trishelle was still pressed against the wall as he caged her in with his body and handed her the surprisingly still-warm cup.

"I had planned to bring you coffee and make you breakfast. Had Marguerite make it extra hot so that it was still drinkable when I brought it to you," he said before taking a sip of his coffee.

"Not afraid I'll throw this in your face?" she asked before taking a sip.

It was still a little too hot, but it helped to further calm her nerves. It also helped his case that he had known her usual coffee order, but then again, he could have just asked Marguerite what it was. While Santa's Workshop had a perfectly good coffee maker, Ma and Pa Freeman only knew how to make two types of coffee. Jet fuel and Jet fuel plus.

"I might tease you, little elf, but I know you save most of your naughty habits for between the sheets," he smirked.

Was he really trying to flirt his way out of this? It was kind of working, so she forced herself to think about him shifting and that got her back to that sweet spot between sheer panic and clear skepticism.

"So, uh, this mate business?" she squeaked.

"What about it?"

"How exactly does it work?"

He studied her for a moment, clearly choosing his words carefully. "That depends," he replied.

"On what?"

"You."

"Me?"

"Yeah, you. I'm a shifter, as you now know, so for me it means I am very serious about this being a forever-after situation."

"Oh," she said, not sure how she should respond to that, even as butterflies fluttered in her stomach and her heart raced. Her brain was sending all sorts of red flag warnings.

"Just oh?"

"What? Did you expect some declaration of love?"

"Not in the slightest, and to be honest, I'm not there yet either. I will be though, real soon now that I've tasted you. It's in my biology. Not very romantic, huh?"

"No, it isn't," she agreed.

"That's why I was slow walking this. I was going to get you comfortable with the boyfriend title, and when I felt you were ready, I was going to ease you into this whole shifter business. I mean, you would have had to know anyway if you planned to stick around Santana," he said, still eyeing her as if he was afraid she would bolt at any second.

She wasn't going to. At least, not yet. She was still trying to process it all. It was completely unfair she had to do so when her body still ached from all the delicious ways he'd worked her flesh the night before. There were two things she was clear on. The first was that she wasn't leaving her dream job based on the information given. Knowing that the people she worked with were also the animals she worked with cleared up a lot of coincidences she hadn't been able to explain otherwise. The second was that she was still very much attracted to Jesse Freeman, despite having every reason not to be.

"You still with me, love?"

"Don't call me love."

"Okay, do you have any more questions for me? I can give you some time to gather your thoughts if you need," he said.

"You didn't finish explaining the whole mate thing. At least, not my role in that."

"To be honest, it's not much different from falling in love the usual way, I guess. At least, for you. Just different terms are used and some slightly different mechanics to the commitment aspect."

"Like what? Do you have to bite me or is blood sharing involved? Do you have some sort of pheromone that can't be simply washed away?" Trishelle was genuinely curious about that part, regardless of her decision to pursue a relationship with Jesse or not.

"I nibbled on you all last night, got a taste of your blood from some of those splinter holes on your ass, and you most certainly are covered in my scent right now, but none of that means anything you don't want it to mean. If and when you are ready to commit to me, I'll buy you whatever ring you want and we'll plan the ceremony of your dreams, just like any other guy worth his salt would give to the woman he loves," he replied.

"So, the romance novels are wrong about that, huh," she shrugged.

Jesse laughed, "That's what you were basing your facts on? Fiction books? I guess I shouldn't be surprised, but hell, if that's what you want, sweetheart, I can play the dashing rogue, the impassioned suitor, the beast to your beauty. I might not have a castle, but I've got a secluded cabin outside a fairytale village full of helpful little critters that I could offer you to escape the harsh realities of the real world."

Trishelle kissed him before he could continue. He hesitated for a moment before pressing his body into hers and deepening the kiss.

"I don't need a Prince Charming," Trishelle said when he finally came up for air.

"No? What do you need, my little elf?"

"I'm not sure exactly and this is probably a bad idea, but I want to be your naughty elf. At least for today and maybe for longer, at least until I work this attraction for you out of my system and can finally think rationally about all of this," she rushed out.

"I think I can handle that," Jesse said and lifted her into his arms before carrying her out of Santa's Workshop.

All I Want for Christmas Is You

Jesse

Big fluffy snowflakes drifted down and landed in freezing wet clumps on Trishelle's face. She turned her head up to the sky and stuck her tongue out to catch them like a little kid. She looked beautiful in her red crushed velvet elf suit with white faux fur accents. A striking contrast to the overcast sky, frosted forest, and shimmering ice on the ground.

If you had told Jesse six months ago that by Christmas, not only would he be preparing a surprise Christmas commitment ceremony complete with an officiant dressed as Santa but his non-committed ass would be the groom, he'd have laughed you out of Santana. Yet, here he was, watching his unknowing future wife enjoying the snow while he prepped the sleigh that would take them from the cabin she'd helped him finish renovating into their new home and on to the town square where the whole town was waiting to see them pledge forever. That is, if she said yes and didn't kick his ass for lying about waiting until she told him she was ready, even though she'd already told Shayla who immediately offered to help him get this plan worked out without Trishelle finding out.

"You ready, love?" he called.

Trishelle stopped spinning and turned a radiant grin toward him. "Of course! I finally get to drive the sleigh!"

He snorted and nodded for her to come on. His young family members who waited patiently in their reindeer form for the honor of driving the bride to the event, already knew the deal. She would have the reins in her hands, but they would be doing all the work of making sure they got safely down to the center of town at a moderate pace.

Trishelle happily climbed into the sleigh, and Jesse handed her the reins.

"Remember what I taught you. A light flick of the wrist to get them started, and a slow and steady pull on the side you want them to turn. No sharp or quick movements and always keep your eyes on where you're going. Pull both reins at the same time to slow them to a stop," he reminded her.

The snow had been unexpected, but the trail was still clear enough that he didn't have to disappoint Trishelle right before the big surprise. Still, he gripped the edge of the seat tight as she flicked her wrists and the team lurched forward. Trishelle shrieked and giggled with excitement, but suddenly, Jesse wasn't feeling all that great. He'd underestimated his nerves of steel that now felt weaker than ramen noodles sitting too long in hot water.

"How am I doing?" Trishelle asked a few minutes later.

"Just great, love. You're doing great!" he said, hoping he sounded convincing, but she shot him a look that told him he absolutely did not before she grinned again.

"Oh look! Everyone's gathered by the fountain. I wonder what's going on?" she said, slowing the team as they hit the asphalt road of Main Street.

Jesse had known he should have come up with some cover story for why everyone would gather at the fountain on Christmas day when they would usually be busy tending to the tourists flocking to their businesses, but it was too late for that now.

"Why don't we go check it out? Might be something important," he said.

Trishelle looked at him suspiciously before stopping the sleigh altogether before they reached the crowd gathered at the fountain.

"All right, what's going on? First, you were singing All I Want for Christmas is You while in the shower. Then, you made me Christmas tree-shaped cinnamon swirl pancakes for breakfast. Plus, this surprise, letting me drive the sleigh when just last week you claimed it would only happen over your dead body."

Jesse smirked. Yeah, he was caught, but he should have known Trishelle would catch on that he hadn't been in his usual grinch mode this Christmas. "Maybe your holiday cheer rubbed off on me."

"Jesse, you live in the most holiday cheer environment in the world and you think I'm going to believe I changed that after years of you being the town grinch?"

"Maybe falling in love with you grew my heart from three sizes too small to three sizes bigger than them all."

"Oh my god! Do reindeer get heartworm? Are you dying?" she shrieked, jumping into his arms.

"What? No. I mean, yes, reindeer can get arterial worms, but no, I don't have them and I am not dying. Woman, I'm trying to be romantic," he laughed.

Trishelle smiled wide and booped his nose. "Aww! Are you trying to make this Christmas extra special since it's my first in Santana?"

"Yes, now can we please continue with this carefully planned date?"

She nodded excitedly and grabbed the reins once more.

Trishelle

Her heart was racing in her chest, and she couldn't shake the feeling there was much more to Jesse's surprise romantic Christmas date. Both he and Shayla had been acting strange for weeks, which didn't exactly mean it had anything to do with her. Shayla was heavily pregnant, due any day now, and things with her and her two beaus weren't exactly settled.

This was also admittedly not Jesse's favorite time of year, but he was trying hard not to ruin it for her. She'd adjusted pretty quickly to the idea of him and his family being reindeer shifters, but it still tripped her up a few times around town when she couldn't tell which animals were actual animals and which were shifters. There was also the Fae, the vampires, and the witches. Needless to say, Santana was full of more than just the magic of Christmas.

None of that had stopped her from falling head over heels for Jesse and the quirky little town. When she'd finally been able to reach her parents on their satellite phone, they'd been happy she'd finally found a place where she fit in without compromising who she was. They'd said they couldn't make it in time to visit for Christmas but that New

Year's might be doable. Trishelle couldn't wait to share the magic with them too.

The snow had slowed and stopped by the time they reached town and the asphalt roads were well-salted, so when she signaled the team to stop in front of the crowd by the fountain, they stopped with a small jolt. Jesse scowled a little, not at her but at the team. She knew he'd spent a lot of time training them how to make everything look smooth and effortless, and she cringed thinking about how he was going to "retrain" the young shifters later.

"We made it!" she said brightly.

Jesse stopped glaring at the team to smile at her before taking her hand. "You did great."

"So, does this mean I get to drive the sleigh next year?" she pushed.

He snorted, "Nope, this was a one-time deal. A first Christmas special."

He climbed down from the sleigh before offering her his hand again to help her down. Once on the ground, the crowd of locals parted, revealing that the fountain, while not currently running, was filled with poinsettias. Her favorite flower.

"Oh my god! It's beautiful!" Trishelle gushed.

"You're beautiful," Jesse said, but instead of his voice coming from above on her right side, it sounded like he was closer to the ground.

She turned to see Jesse on one knee looking nervous as hell as he held out an open red jewelry box. Inside, a ring with red ruby petals surrounding a trio of diamonds in the center mimicked the look of a poinsettia.

"Oh my god, Jesse! Are you?"

"Yes, I am. Trishelle Monet Harris, will you marry me?"

"You're serious," she gasped, still in shock.

"As a heart attack," he said.

She hesitated for a second longer before kissing him with a resounding, "Yes!"

"Oh, thank god!" She vaguely heard Shayla say from the crowd. Trishelle was too busy kissing her new fiancé to care that they had the whole town as an audience.

She eventually had to come up for air, and Jesse slid the gorgeous ring on her finger.

"This is officially my favorite Christmas," she said.

Jesse smiled down at her. "Oh, I'm not done yet, love."

He stepped away and waved his hand. The crowd parted again and her parents emerged from the crowd, along with Jesse's father dressed as Santa.

"Mom, Dad? I thought you couldn't make it!"

She was officially crying now. She probably looked a whole mess with glitter and mascara running down her face, but she didn't care. She was so happy.

"You think we'd miss your Christmas wedding?" Her mother laughed.

"Yeah, I wasn't going to miss walking my baby down the aisle," her father cosigned.

"Wait, what? We just got engaged, we aren't..." She whirled around to Jesse who stood there grinning from ear to ear.

"Surprise!"

That was when Shayla and Jesse's mom stepped forward. Shayla had a crystal-studded elf hat in her hand, and Ma held what looked like the same Hungarian lace veil Trishelle had admired in the older woman's wedding photos.

"Do you mind? I'd love it if you'd wear my veil for the ceremony," Ma said, tears in her eyes.

"I'd be honored," Trishelle sobbed and hugged her future mother-in-law.

Within seconds, she was swarmed by the women in Jesse's family as they fussed and prodded her into bridal glory. Shayla swapped out her elf hat and attempted to fix Trishelle's makeup while Ma pinned the long veil into place. One of Jesse's cousins had appeared with a belted tulle skirt that added a bridal train to her elf suit. When they were done, they stepped back and Trishelle's mom stepped forward holding her grandmother's Christmas brooch. It was a family heirloom passed down through the matriarchs of her family and only worn on Christmas day as they hosted the family's annual gathering for the holiday.

"I should have gifted this to you sooner, but today couldn't be a more perfect time," her mother said.

Trishelle made a mess of her makeup all over again as her mother pinned the brooch to her lapel before hugging her tight. Then her father came up, kissed her cheek, and tucked her arm into the crook of his elbow.

"Do I need to run you out of here? I've got the car still idling in case this isn't what you want," he whispered.

"Thank you, Daddy, but this is everything I didn't know I wanted until now," she assured him.

"All right, but if this mate business turns out not to be what you expected, I'm only a call away," he said.

She froze and looked up at her father. His eyes twinkled as he urged her forward. His choice to use the word mate was not a coincidence, and now Trishelle was curious as to what all Jesse had told her parents when he'd obviously planned for them to be here. Her curiosity would have to wait, however, as her father walked her the short distance through the parted crowd to the fountain where Jesse waited in a green suit jacket over a white button-down and black slacks. His own eyes glistened with tears as he looked her up and down. His father stood by his side dressed in full Santa regalia and holding an old Bible in his palm.

This was officially the Christmas of all Christmases in Trishelle's book.

Santa Baby

Shayla

Shayla watched with tears in her eyes as Jesse and Trishelle kissed for the first time as husband and wife. She was exceedingly happy for her friend and her brother but also a little jealous. She searched the crowd for the two men who held her heart and her happiness captive but didn't see either of them.

Her gut clenched and her hand went instinctively to her belly. She still hadn't told the rest of the family about her pregnancy, despite being due any day now. Her plan to spill the beans at Thanksgiving had been ruined by Jesus and Terry having another big public fight over her, and in her anger, she had told them both they could kick rocks.

With Jesus' glamour still in place, no one but her and the people who already knew she was pregnant could see her belly, but that wasn't going to be much help soon. Very soon, judging by the increased intensity of her Braxton Hicks contractions. The next one that hit had her bending over and biting back a groan. Yeah, this baby wasn't going to be in there for much longer. She waddled away from the crowd, ignoring the concerned looks from her family and a few of the townspeople who had noticed her weird behavior.

She just needed to make it to the park bench a few feet away. Once she sat, it would be easier to enjoy the moment without drawing attention to herself as she breathed through the false contraction. Only, she didn't quite make it to the bench before the next contraction hit and this one was a big one. She groaned aloud as her belly tightened, and she felt her water burst, fluid gathering at her crotch, making it look like she'd just peed her pants.

"Shit, shit shit!" she cursed.

She waddled further from the crowd. Her intent was to make it to the bench but instead, the contractions were too strong. She doubled over as another contraction hit, this one so intense her vision blurred. Then suddenly, she was being lifted by a familiar pair of muscular arms.

"I've got you, Shay Baby," Terry said.

Her vision cleared as the contraction passed, and Terry lifted her into the sleigh that had brought Jesse and Trishelle to town. And he didn't just lift her, but handed her to Jesus who had appeared out of nowhere.

"We've got you, love," Jesus said.

Her young cousins, still in reindeer form, gave her weird looks.

"Don't look at me like that. Take me to the hospital," she snapped at them.

They snorted and kicked at the icy ground while Terry climbed into the sleigh next to her and Jesus.

"You heard the lady, get moving!" he barked, and they took off at a sprint.

Also By Stella Williams

<u>Sowell Gate Universe</u>
Wild Cross Family

Felling Bechet

Yarding Braxton

Branding Baron

Reclaiming Hunter
Monsters & Mayhem

Peak
Unforgettable Holiday Romance

Unforgettable Valentine
Unforgettable Christmas
Brimstone

Fire and Brimstone

Song and Brimstone

Alchemy and Brimstone

Shadow and Brimstone

<u>Maura's Men Universe</u>
Bloodlines

His Soul To Keep

To Catch Akellah
Secret of Ceres

Ferocious

Dauntless

Earnest

Zenith
Langsmith Shifters

Coy Wolf

A Night Divine

Bird of Prey
Maura's Men

Xander's Claim

Claude's Conquest

Shane's Redemption

www.ingramcontent.com/pod-product-compliance
Lightning Source LLC
Chambersburg PA
CBHW030906200726
48289CB00003B/925